The Wind That Wanted to Rest

Sheldon Oberman

Illustrated by Neil Waldman

Afterword by Peninnah Schram

BOYDS MILLS PRESS

HONESDALE, PENNSYLVANIA

Boyds Mills Press, Inc.
815 Church Street
Honesdale, Pennsylvania
Printed in China

ISBN: 978-1-59078-858-5
Library of Congress Control Number: 2011940126
First edition
The text of this book is set in 16-point ITC Berkeley Oldstyle.
The illustrations are done in watercolors.

10 9 8 7 6 5 4 3 2 1

For my late husband, Obie (Sheldon), whose stories live
on in our hearts and in the pages of this book
—LD

For my dear friends Liliya and Leonid Klevitsky
—NW

A winter wind was searching the world for a place to rest. He was an old and tired winter wind who had spent his life rushing here, there, and everywhere across the earth.

He came to a town with thick walls and towers. "This is a fine place to rest," he said, and he swooped down to the streets. He slid his cold fingers against the windowpanes, making beautiful designs. He whistled his weary wind song into chimneys high and low. He settled with a sigh in a cozy spot between a bakery and a blacksmith shop.

Then the baker built a fire in his oven. The walls grew warm. The windows opened, blowing out hot, dry air. The baker shouted, "Bread for sale! Cakes and cookies fresh from the oven!"

The blacksmith started a fire in his forge. He heated iron rods and beat them with a hammer into horseshoes. *Boom* and *bang! Clang* and *clatter!*

"The town is full of heat and noise," the wind moaned. "It's no place for a tired winter wind."

He left the town and came to a meadow, where he found a stand of oak trees. "I'll wrap myself around these trees and I won't wander anymore," said the wind. He swept and swirled and settled in.

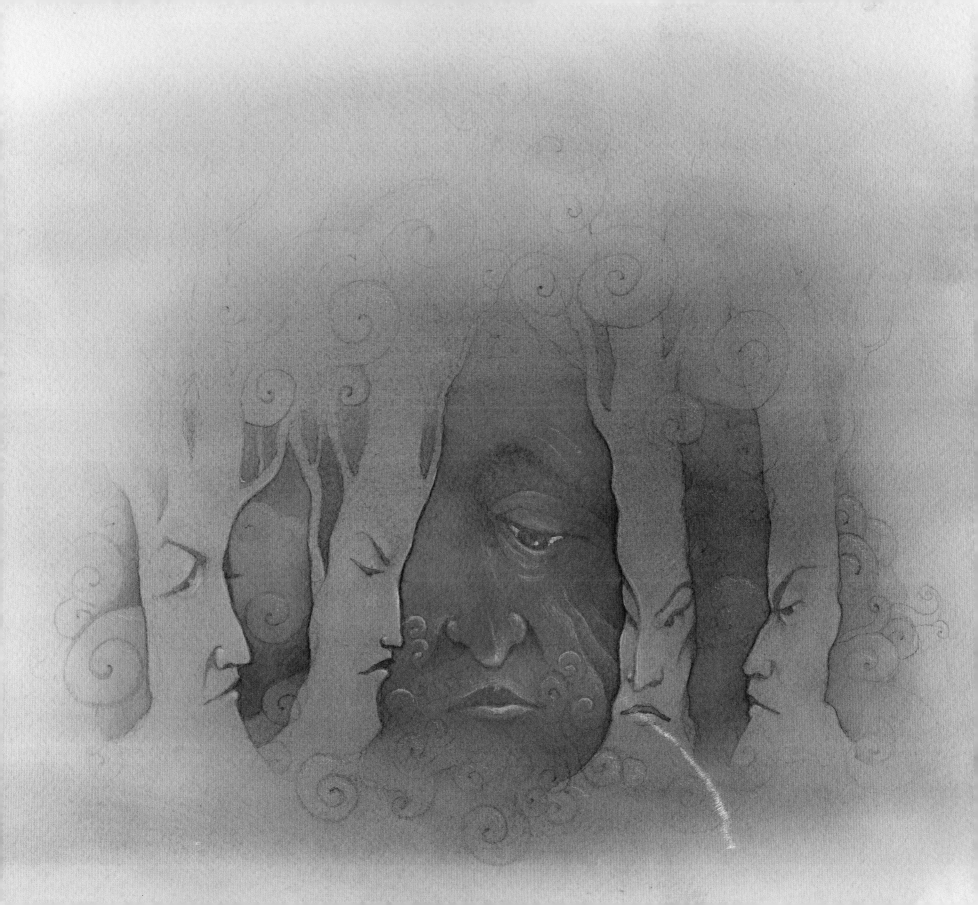

"Who are you?" the oak trees groaned. "You'll blow away our blanket of snow. Get off our roots, or they will freeze and we will die!"

"I'm sorry, trees," the old wind whispered. "I just need a place to rest."

"Not here!" the oak trees creaked. "Go away! Leave us alone!"

And so the old wind searched again until he saw a mountain. "That's where I'll make my bed," he said, "far from harm and worry." He settled into the mountaintop, but just as he was slipping into sleep, he heard a rumble.

"Who are you?" the mountain asked. "What are you doing in my cracks and crannies?"

"Sleeping, only sleeping," said the wind. "I'm an old winter wind. I cannot hurt you."

"Spring is coming," said the mountain. "The rain will fill my cracks. You will freeze the rain to ice. Then the ice will break and split me into stones. Stone by stone, I'll tumble down."

"I just need a place to rest," the old wind whispered.

"Go away!" the mountain rumbled.

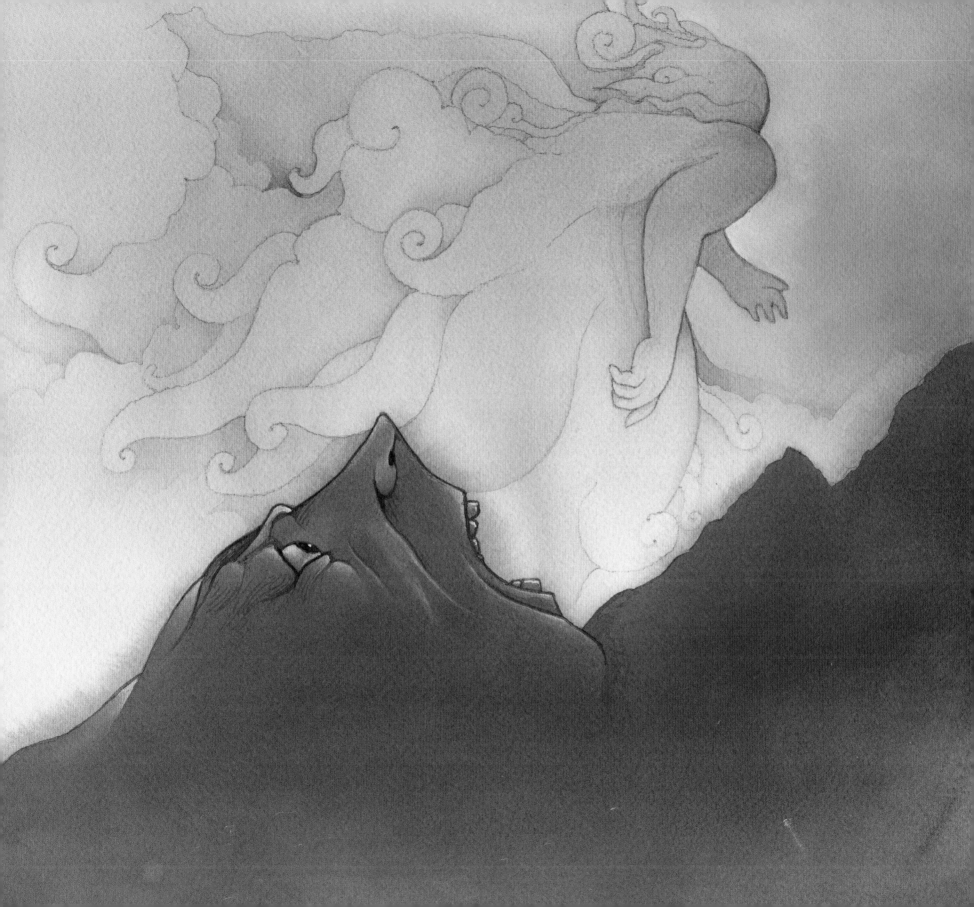

By now, the wind was too tired to travel through the sky. He drifted along a country road, turning this way and that. At the end of the day, he came to an inn for travelers. "Perhaps there's room inside for me," he said as he entered through the open door.

The travelers began to cry, "There's a draft, a breeze, a cold wind blowing!"

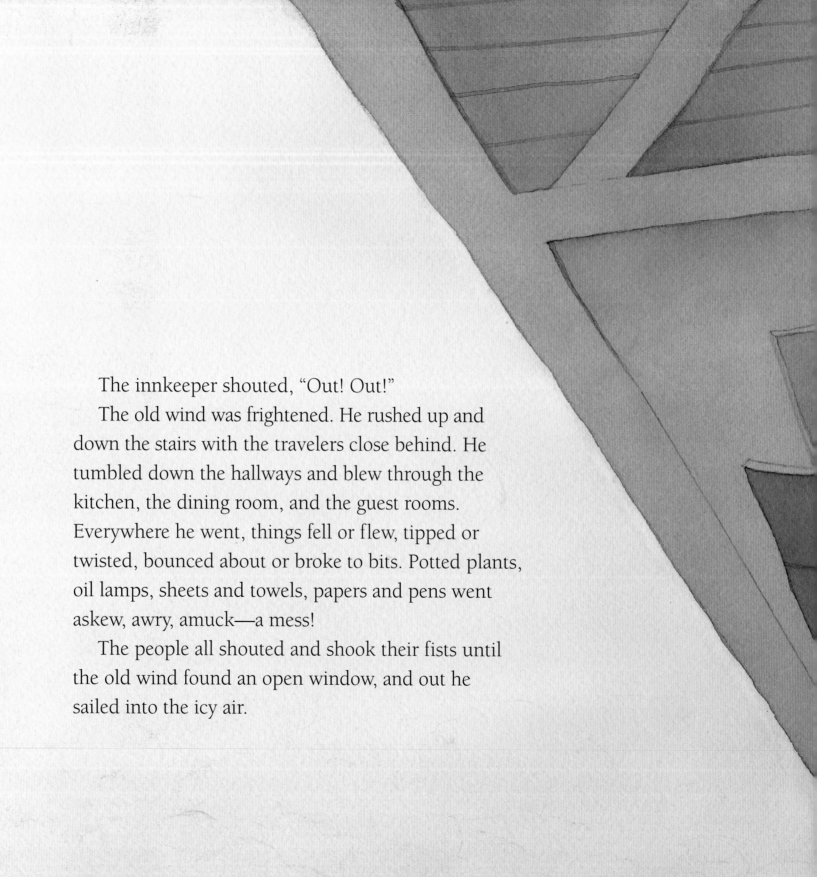

The innkeeper shouted, "Out! Out!"

The old wind was frightened. He rushed up and down the stairs with the travelers close behind. He tumbled down the hallways and blew through the kitchen, the dining room, and the guest rooms. Everywhere he went, things fell or flew, tipped or twisted, bounced about or broke to bits. Potted plants, oil lamps, sheets and towels, papers and pens went askew, awry, amuck—a mess!

The people all shouted and shook their fists until the old wind found an open window, and out he sailed into the icy air.

"No one cares!" the wind cried.

Suddenly, he forgot that he was old. He forgot that he was tired. He grew angry at the world. He grew bigger with every breath till he was a storming giant.

"No one cares!" he shouted and blew.

He raised the snow up from the fields. He pulled the clouds down from the sky. He raged against the inns and the trees and the mountains and the towns.

"No one cares!" he roared.

Snow darkened the sky. When it fell, it buried the earth and clogged the roads and rivers. One by one, the lights of the towns and roadside inns went dark as snow rose past the windows, creeping up to the roofs. Still, the old winter wind raged on.

Merchants, farmers, soldiers in their forts, sailors in their ships at sea shouted at the wind. "You wicked wind! You should not and you must not storm at us. You have to stop!"

The wind grew angrier and blew their words away.

Mothers called to the wind, "Strong wind, great wind, look what you are doing. You're frightening and freezing us. Please stop!"

"No one cares!" the wind bellowed.

The old wind cried tears of ice and rain, until the trees bent to the ground. The mountain began to creak and crack. Its stones began to slip and slide.

In the midst of the storm, the wind heard a small voice. "Poor wind. Sad wind. What's the matter?"

The wind stopped howling to see who had spoken. It was a girl outside a farmhouse, far from the rest of the world.

"I am an old and tired wind," he whispered. "I just need a place to rest."

"I'll take care of you," said the girl. "We have a dark, dry, quiet place underneath our house. Once it held our vegetables and firewood, but we don't use it anymore. Rest there, old winter wind. Stay as long as you want."

"You are very kind," he said. Then the old winter wind slipped into the space beneath the house. He was not sad or angry any longer.

One morning, as winter turned to spring, the wind awoke. Saying good-bye to the girl, he soared into the sky. The girl watched as the old wind grew smaller and smaller, finally disappearing behind a mountaintop. He was never seen again. But he had left the girl a gift. From that day on, the cellar was always full of fresh, clean snow, enough snow to keep the girl and her family cool and laughing throughout the hottest summers.

Afterword

Stories transcend time and place and are passed on from generation to generation. The storyteller who wrote down this tale, "The Wind That Wanted to Rest," while no longer in this world, still lives through the stories he told and recorded in written form. Sheldon Oberman (1949–2004) understood the power of telling the tale. He had a talent for telling a story, not as a literary work but as part of the oral tradition—even when the story was transformed into a book. His written stories maintain a dynamic oral quality. The words, the alliteration, the dialogue, the images, the sounds, and the colors are rich and appear in a many-splendored Technicolor mosaic.

When Sheldon Oberman wrote "The Wind That Wanted to Rest," he gave it the subtitle "A Jewish Tale from Soviet Russia." However, in my search for its origins, I could not find this particular story or variant, not even in the Israel Folktale Archives. So I am uncertain whether this is a story someone told him or whether it is partly original in nature.

The personification of the wind is a motif that appears in Jewish folktales[1] as well as in folktales from Lithuania, a country that borders Russia. In fact, this motif is found in the myths and folktales of many cultures. Wind gods and goddesses appear in the writings of Aesop and Ovid and in the ancient myths of people as far apart as the Celts and Maya.

In the Jewish tradition, there is a legend of King Solomon in which the wind grabs a sack of flour out of a poor woman's hands to plug a hole in a sinking boat. In the end, the woman is identified and receives a reward from the grateful men on the ship.[2] Centuries later, in "Ode to the West Wind," Percy Bysshe Shelley addressed the wind as though it were a person, calling it "Wild Spirit." Later still, S. Y. Agnon wrote "From Foe to Friend."[3] In this story, the wind has ruled for years in a certain area of Jerusalem and resents a man who attempts to build a shelter there. Finally, the wind and the man teach each other an important lesson and become respectful and peaceful neighbors.

Oberman's tale also shows the powerful role of the wind. At first, we meet an "old and tired winter wind" searching for a place to rest. But wherever the wind stops, he is spurned and rejected. The wind becomes increasingly angry and summons up disastrous force. In a moving finale, a compassionate child offers the old wind a place where he can sleep. When the wind leaves in the spring, the child discovers that he has left a legacy that is useful and beautiful. In one brief story, through the character of the wind that embodies human qualities, we can see how our actions and treatment of others can cause rippling effects, either positive or destructive, out in the world.

—*Peninnah Schram*

1. Identified by folklorist Dov Noy in Stith Thompson's *Motif-Index of Folk-Literature*, rev. ed. (Bloomington: Indiana University Press, 1960).

2. Peninnah Schram, "The Flour and the Wind" in *The Hungry Clothes and Other Jewish Folktales* (New York: Sterling Publishing, 2008).

3. *The Jerusalem Post*, August 1, 1958, viii.